Rocking
Horse
Land

for Wendy

who left us
(and this book)
much, much
too soon

ROCKING HORSE LAND
AND OTHER
CLASSIC TALES OF DOLLS AND TOYS

COMPILED
BY
NAOMI
LEWIS

PICTURES
BY
ANGELA
BARRETT

CANDLEWICK PRESS
CAMBRIDGE, MASSACHUSETTS

INTRODUCTION

Looking about, in street or shop, I almost never see a very young child without a doll or toy or other favored object. What is the child's relationship to the toy? Not at all what adults might casually think. No, the bond between child and doll is not a simple one. First of all, the child is not the parent of the doll, nor is the doll the child of the child. Indeed, for the very young, the doll or toy can be the first really private and personal friend and ally. A year or two later, the doll might be both playmate and confidant in a problematic world, as much for a child with too many brothers and sisters as for an "only." In this alliance is also a hint of those later child-and-child friendships, so close and perfect while they last.

In my own childhood experience (there were four of us: boy, girl, girl, boy) dolls had a serious place. A new doll or toy, arriving from this or that donor, for this or that child, would be gazed at by all, given a name, then would take its place in the curious ten-and-under world. My "best" doll, to whom

I had given the exotic name of Joan, perished through serving too often as the sheeted corpse of Caesar to my older brother's Mark Antony. My sister and I were always the Citizens, one-word parts that have always remained for me potent and meaningful.

There comes a time when the magic two-way link between child and doll grows thin. But it does not go; it simply moves into other paths of the mind. (Remember the search for Rosebud in "Citizen Kane"?) Writers have a particular chance of following these paths, as, in their very different ways, the stories here will show. Reading the tin soldier story, we share his steadfast courage in love and in every kind of danger. Listening to the wise toy mouse, we learn an amazing yet simple secret worth remembering in daily life. As for the doll of Vasilissa, she is the one that we would all wish to possess, the doll who solves all of our difficulties.

Child-scale, doll-scale, the problems of life do not alter. Every child doll-owner lives through more woes and wonders than so many unremembering adults will guess. Am I not right?

Naomi Lewis

CONTENTS

The Memoirs of a London Doll

Mrs. Fairstar

This story is the opening episode of THE MEMOIRS OF A LONDON DOLL (1846). A *superb doll classic, it is not only a captivating story but a vivid document about child life at different social levels in the earliest years of Queen Victoria's reign. The author, Richard Henry (or "Hengist") Horne — alias "Mrs. Fairstar" — was a friend of Charles Dickens, Henry Mayhew, Mark Lemon, and Elizabeth Barrett Browning, who all in their writing drew attention to the lives of the working or workless poor. Horne himself (1803–84) had served as government investigator into conditions of child labor in mills and factories. But because he was writing a book for children's pleasure he never overstressed the hardships in this tale. Unforgettable is the spirited verbal contest between the doll seller with his splendid doll and the pastry maker's grandson with his splendid cake.*

In a large dusky room at the top of a dusky house in one of the dusky streets of High Holborn, there lived a poor doll maker, whose name was Sprat. He was an extremely small man for his age, and not altogether unlike  a sprat in the face. He was always dressed in a sort of tight pinafore and trousers, all in one, that fitted close to his body; and this dress was nearly covered with dabs of paint, especially white paint, of which he used most in his work. His family consisted of his wife, and three children — two boys and a girl.

This poor family had but one room, which was at the top of the house. It had no ceiling, but only beams and tiles. It was the workshop by day and the bedroom at night. In the morning, as the children lay in bed, looking up, they could see the light through the chinks in the tiles; and when they went to bed in the evening they could often feel the wind come down, and breathe its cool breath under their nightcaps. Along the wall on one side of the room, farthest from the windows, the beds were laid upon the floor; the largest was for the poor sprat-faced doll maker and his wife, the next largest was for the two boys, and the smallest, up in the corner, was for the little girl. There were two windows opposite; and a wooden bench, like a long kitchen dresser, extended from one side of the room to the other, close to these windows. Here all the work was done.

This bench was covered with all manner of things; such as little wooden legs and arms, and wooden heads without hair, and small bodies, and half legs and half arms, which had not yet been fitted together in the joints, and paint pots and painting brushes, and bits of paper and rags of all colors; and there were tools for cutting and polishing, and very small hammers, and several old pillboxes full of little wooden pegs, and corners of scouring paper, and small wooden boxes and trays full of little glass eyes, and glue pots and bits of wax and bits of leather, and a small red pipkin for melting wax, and another for melting India rubber, and a broken teacup for varnish, and several tiny round bladders, and tiny tin boxes, all full of things very precious to Mr. Sprat in his business.

All the family worked at doll making, and were very industrious. Mr. Sprat was of course the great manager and doer of most things, and always the finisher, but Mrs. Sprat was also clever in her department, which was entirely that of the *eyes*. She either painted the eyes, or else, for the superior class of dolls, fitted in the glass ones. She, moreover, always painted the eyebrows, and was so used to it, that she could make exactly the same sort of arch

when it was late in the evening and nearly dark, before candles were lighted. The eldest boy painted hair; or fitted and glued hair onto the heads of the best dolls. The second boy fitted half legs and arms together, by pegs at the joints. The little girl did nothing but paint rosy cheeks and lips, which she always did very nicely, though sometimes she made them rather too red, and looking as if very hot, or blushing extremely.

Now Mr. Sprat was very ingenious and clever in his business as a doll maker. He was able to make dolls of various kinds, even of wax, or of a sort of composition; and sometimes he did make a few of such materials; but his usual business was to make jointed dolls — dolls who could move their legs and arms in many positions — and these were of course made of wood. Of this latter material I was manufactured.

The first thing I recollect of myself was a kind of a pegging, and pushing, and scraping, and twisting, and tapping down of both sides of me, above and below. These latter operations were the fitting on of my legs and arms. Then, I passed into the hands of the most gentle of all the Sprat family, and felt something delightfully warm laid upon my cheeks and mouth. It was the little girl who was painting me a pair of rosy cheeks and lips; and her face, as she bent over me, was the first object of life that my eyes distinctly saw. The face was a smiling one, and as I looked up at it I tried to smile too, but I felt some hard material over the outside of my face, which my smile did not seem to be able to get through, so I do not think the little girl perceived it.

But the last thing done to me was by Mr. Sprat himself, whose funny white face and round eyes I could now see. He turned me about and about in his hands, examining and trying my legs and arms, which he moved backward and forward, and up and down, to my great terror, and fixed my limbs in various attitudes. I was so frightened! I thought he would break something off me. However, nothing happened, and when he was satisfied that I was a complete doll in all parts, he hung me up on a line that ran along the room overhead, extending from one wall to the other, and near to the two beams that also extended from wall to wall.

I hung upon the line to dry, in company with many other dolls, both boys and girls, but mostly girls. The tops of the beams were also covered with dolls, all of whom, like those on the lines, were waiting there till their paint or varnish had properly dried and hardened. I passed the time in observing what was going on in the room under my line, and also the contents of the room, not forgetting my numerous little companions, who were all smiling and staring, or sleeping, round about me.

Mr. Sprat was a doll maker only; he never made dolls' clothes. He said *that* was not work for an artist like him. So in about a week, when I was properly dry, and the varnish of my complexion thoroughly hardened and like enamel, Mr. Sprat took me down — examined me all over for the last time — and then, nodding his head to himself several times, with a face of seriousness and satisfaction, as much as to say, "You are a doll fit in all respects for the most polished society" — he handed me to his wife, who wrapped me up in silver paper, all but the head, and laying me in a basket among nine others papered up in the same way, she carried me off to a large doll shop not far from the corner of New Turnstile in High Holborn.

I arrived safe at the doll shop, and Mrs. Sprat took me out of the basket with her finger and thumb, keeping all her other fingers spread out, for fear of soiling my silver paper.

"Place all these dolls on the shelf in the back parlor," said the master of the shop. "I have no room yet for them in the window." As I was carried to the shelf I caught a glimpse of the shop window! What a bright

and confused sensation it gave me! Everything seemed so light and merry and numerous! And then, through all this crowd of many shapes and colors, packed and piled and hanging up in the window, I saw the crowds of large walking people passing outside in the world, which was as yet perfectly unknown to me! Oh how I longed to be placed in the shop window! I felt I should learn things so fast, if I could only see them. But I was placed in a dark box, among a number of other dolls, for a long time, and when I was taken out I was laid upon my back upon a high shelf, with my rosy cheeks and blue eyes turned toward the ceiling.

Yet I cannot say that the time I passed on this shelf was by any means lost or wasted. I thought of all I had seen in Mr. Sprat's room, and all I had heard them talk about, which gave me many very strange and serious thoughts about the people who lived in the world only for the purpose, as I supposed, of buying dolls. The conversation of Mr. Sprat with his family made me very naturally think this; and in truth I have never since been quite able to fancy but that the principal business of mankind was that of buying and selling dolls and toys.

What I heard the master of the shop in Holborn often say, helped to fix this early impression on my mind.

But the means by which I learned very much of other things and other thoughts, was by hearing the master's little girl Emmy read aloud to her elder sister. Emmy read all sorts of pretty books, every word of which I eagerly listened to, and felt so much interested, and so delighted, and so anxious and curious to hear more. She read pretty stories of little boys and girls, and affectionate mammas and aunts, and kind old nurses, and birds in the fields and woods, and flowers in the gardens and hedges; and then such beautiful fairy tales; and also pretty stories in verse; all of which gave me great pleasure, and were indeed my earliest education. There was the lovely book called *Birds and Flowers,* by Mary Howitt; the nice stories about Willie, by Mrs. Marcett; the delightful little books of Mrs. Harriet Myrtle — in which I did *so* like to hear about old Mr. Dove, the village carpenter, and little Mary, and the account of May Day, and the Day in the Woods — and besides other books, there was oh! *such* a story book called *The Good-natured Bear*! But I never heard any stories about dolls, and what they thought, or what happened to them! This rather disappointed me. Living at a doll shop, and hearing the daughter of the master of such a wonderful shop reading so often, I naturally expected to have heard more about dolls than any other creatures! However, on the whole, I was very well contented, and should have been perfectly happy if they would only have hung me up in the shop window! What I wanted was to be placed in the bright window, and to look into the astonishing street!

Soon after this, however, by a fortunate accident, I was moved to an upright position with my back against a doll's cradle, so that I could look down into the room below, and see what was going on there.

How long I remained upon the shelf I do not know, but it seemed like years to me, and I learned a great deal.

One afternoon Emmy had been reading to her sister as usual, but this time the story had been about a great Emperor in France who, once upon a time, had a great many soldiers to play with, and whose name was Napoleon Bonaparte. The master himself listened to this, and as he walked thoughtfully up and down from the back room to the shop in front, he made himself a cocked hat of brown paper, and put it upon his head, with the corners pointing to each shoulder. Emmy continued to read, and the master continued thoughtfully walking up and down with his hands behind him, one hand holding the other.

But presently, and when his walk had led him into the front shop, where I could not see him, the shop bell rang and Emmy ceased reading. A boy had come in, and the following dialogue took place.

"If you please, sir," said the voice of the boy, "do you want a nice Twelfth-cake?"

"Not particularly," answered the master, "but I have no objection to one."

"What will you give for it, sir?" said the boy.

"That is quite another question," answered the master. "Go about your business. I am extremely engaged."

"I do not want any money for it, sir," said the boy.

"What do you mean by that, my little captain?" said the master.

"Why, sir," said the boy, "if you please I want a nice doll for my little sister, and I will give you this large Twelfth-cake that I have in paper here for a good doll."

"Let me see the cake," said the master. "So, how did you get this cake?"

"My grandfather is a pastry cook, sir," answered the boy, "and my sister and I live with him. I went today to take home seven Twelfth-cakes. But the family at one house had all gone away out of the country, and locked up the house, and forgotten to send for the cake; and grandfather told me that I and my sister might have it."

"What is your name?"

"Thomas Plummy, sir; and I live in Bishopsgate Street, near the Flower Pot."

"Very well, Thomas Plummy; you may choose any doll you fancy out of that case."

Here some time elapsed; and while the boy was choosing, the master continued his slow walk to and fro from one room to the other, with the brown-paper cocked hat, which he had forgotten to take off, still upon his head. It was so very light that he did not feel it, and did not know it was there. At last the boy declared he did not like any of the dolls in the case, and so went from one case to another, always refusing those the master offered him; and when he did choose one himself the master said it was too expensive. Presently the master said he had another box full of good dolls in the back room, and in he came, looking so grave in his cocked hat, and beginning to open a long wooden box. But the boy had followed him to the door, and peeping in suddenly, called out, "There, sir! That one! That is the doll for my cake!" and he pointed his little brown finger up at me.

"Aha!" said the master, "that one is also too expensive; I cannot let you have that."

However, he took me down, and while the boy was looking at me with evident satisfaction, as if his mind was quite made up, the master got a knife and pushed the point of it into the side of the cake, just to see if it was as good inside as it seemed to be on the

outside. During all this time he never once recollected that he had got on the brown-paper cocked hat.

"Now," said the master, taking me out of the boy's hand, and holding me at arm's length, "you must give me the cake and two shillings besides for this doll. This is a young lady of a very superior make, is this doll. Made by one of the first makers. The celebrated Sprat, the only maker, I may say, of this kind of jointed doll. See! All the joints move – all work in the proper way; up and down, backward and forward, any way you please. See what lovely blue eyes; what rosy cheeks and lips; and what a complexion on the neck, face, hands, and arms! The hair is also of the most beautiful kind of delicate light-brown curl that can possibly be found. You never before saw such a doll, nor any of your relations. It is something, I can tell you, to have such a doll in a family; and if you were to buy her, she would cost you a matter of twelve shillings!"

The boy, without a moment's hesitation, took the cake and held it out flat upon the palm of his hand, balancing it as if to show how heavy it was.

"Sir," said he, "this is a Twelfth-cake, of very superior make. If the young lady who sits reading there was only to taste it, she would say so too. It was made by my grandfather himself, who is known to be one of the first makers in all Bishopsgate Street: I may say the very first. There is no better in all the world. You see how heavy it is; what a quantity of plums, currants, butter, sugar, and orange and lemon peel there is in it, besides brandy and caraway comfits. See what a beautiful frost-work of white sugar there is all over the top and sides! See, too, what characters there are, and made in sugar of all colors! Kings and queens in their robes, and lions and dogs, and Swiss cottages in winter, and railway carriages, and girls with tambourines, and a village steeple with a cow looking in at the porch; and all these standing or walking, or dancing upon white sugar, surrounded with curling twists and true lovers' knots in pink and green citron, with damson cheese and black currant paste between. You never saw such a cake before, sir, and I'm sure none of your family ever smelled any cake at all like it. It's quite a nosegay for the Queen Victoria herself; and if you were to buy it at grandfather's shop you would have to pay fifteen shillings and more for it."

"Thomas Plummy!" said the master, looking very earnestly at the boy; "Thomas Plummy! Take the doll, and give me the cake. I only hope it may prove half as good as you say. And it is my opinion that, if you,

Thomas Plummy, should not happen to be sent to New South Wales to bake brown bread, you may some day or other come to be Lord Mayor of London."

"Thank you, sir," said the boy. "How many Abernethy biscuits will you take for your cocked hat?"

The master instantly put his hand up to his head, looking so confused and vexed, and the boy ran laughing out of the shop. At the door he was met by his sister, who had been waiting to receive me in her arms; and they both ran home, the little girl hugging me close to her bosom, and the boy laughing so much at the effect of the cocked hat that he could hardly speak a word all the way.

The Steadfast Tin Soldier

Hans Christian Andersen
Translated by Naomi Lewis

Andersen had a particular gift for cutting dolls, dancers, flowers, and landscapes out of folded paper (open out, and a whole page of dancers appears); you will find such items again and again in his tales. For one sure mark of the Andersen story is the life and personality given to what some might just call "things" — sticks, straw, beetles, eggshells, and of course toys. THE STEADFAST TIN SOLDIER (1838) is a real piece of human drama — love, loss, courage, loyalty, endurance, deadly peril, wild adventure, and the extraordinary return to where all this began. Happy or unhappy ending? You can choose, but I would say, definitely, the first. Andersen's own life (1805–75) might have been one of his own fairy tales. Born very poor in a small far northern country, writing in a language (Danish) that hardly anyone used outside its borders, he became, and remains, perhaps the best-known storytelling writer in the world.

There were once twenty-five tin soldiers; they were all brothers, for they had all been made from the same tin kitchen spoon. Very smart in their red and blue uniforms, they shouldered arms and looked straight before them.

"Tin soldiers!" Those were the first words they heard in this world, when the lid of their box was taken off. A little boy had shouted this, and clapped his hands; they were a birthday present, and now he set them out on the table. Each soldier was exactly like the next, except for one who had only a single leg; he was the last to be molded, and there was not quite enough tin left. Yet he stood just as well on his one leg as the others did on their two — and he is this story's hero.

On the table where they were placed there were many other toys, but the one which everyone noticed first was a paper castle; you could see right into the rooms through its little windows. In the front, some tiny trees were arranged round a piece of mirror, just like a lake; swans made of wax seemed to float on its surface, gazing at their reflection.

The whole effect was quite enchanting — but the prettiest thing in the whole scene was a young girl who stood in the castle's open doorway. She too was cut out of paper, but her gauzy skirt was of finest muslin; a narrow blue ribbon crossed her  shoulder like a scarf, and was held with a glittering spangle quite the size of her face. This charming little creature held both of her arms stretched out, for she was a dancer; indeed, one of her legs was raised so high that the tin soldier could not see it at all. He believed that she had only one leg like himself.

"Now she would be just the right wife for me," he thought. "But she is so grand. She lives in a castle and I have only a box, and there are twenty-five of us in that! It's certainly no place for her. Still, I can try to make her acquaintance." So he lay down full-length behind a snuffbox which was on the table; from there he had

a good view of the little paper dancer, who continued to stand on one leg without losing her balance.

When evening came, all the other tin soldiers were put in their box, and the people of the house went to bed. Now the toys began to have games of their own; they played at visiting, and battles, and going to parties and dances. The tin soldiers rattled in their box, for they wanted to join in, but they couldn't get the lid off. The nutcrackers turned somersaults and the slate pencil squeaked on the slate; there was such a din that the canary woke up and joined in the talk — what's more, he did it in verse. The only two who didn't move from their places were the tin soldier and the little dancer. She continued to stand on the point of her toe; he stood just as steadily on his single leg, and never once did he take his eyes from her.

Now the clock struck twelve. Crack! The lid flew off the snuffbox, and a little black goblin popped up. There was no snuff inside; it was a toy, a jack-in-the-box.

"Tin soldier!" screeched the goblin. "Keep your eyes to yourself!" But the tin soldier pretended not to hear.

"All right, just you wait till tomorrow!" warned the goblin.

When morning came, and the children were up again, the little boy put the tin soldier on the windowsill. The goblin may have been responsible, or perhaps a draught was blowing through — anyhow, the window suddenly swung open and out fell the tin soldier, all three stories to the ground.

It was a dreadful fall! His leg pointed upward, his head was down, and he came to a halt with his bayonet stuck between the paving stones.

The servant girl and the small boy went out at once to look for the tin soldier, but although they were almost treading on him, they didn't see him. If he had called out, "Here I am!" they would have found him easily, but he didn't think it proper behavior to cry out when in uniform.

It began to rain; the drops fell faster and faster — it was a real drenching storm. When it was over a pair of street urchins passed. "Look!" said one of them. "There's a tin soldier! Let's put him out to sea."

So they made a boat of newspaper, put the tin soldier aboard, and set the boat in the fast-flowing gutter at the edge of the street. Away it sped, and the two boys ran along beside, clapping their hands. Goodness! What waves there were in that gutter stream, what rolling tides! The paper boat tossed up and down, sometimes whirling round and round, until the soldier felt quite giddy. But he remained as steadfast as ever, not moving a muscle, still looking straight in front of him, still shouldering arms.

All at once the boat entered a tunnel under the pavement. Oh, it was dark, dark as it was in the box at home. "Wherever am I going now?" the tin soldier wondered. "Yes, it must be the goblin's doing. Ah, if only that young lady were sharing this journey with me, I wouldn't care if it were twice as dark!"

Suddenly a large water rat rushed out from its home in the tunnel. "Have you a passport?" the rat demanded. "No getting through without a passport!"

But the tin soldier said never a word; he only gripped his musket more tightly than ever. The boat rushed on and the rat chased after it. Ugh! How it ground its teeth and yelled to the sticks and straws, "Stop him! Stop him! He hasn't paid his toll! He hasn't shown his passport!"

There was no stopping him though, for the stream ran stronger and stronger. The tin soldier could see a bright glimpse of daylight ahead where the end of the tunnel must be, but at the same time he heard a roaring noise which well might have frightened a bolder man. Just imagine! At the end of the tunnel

the stream thundered down into a canal. It was as fearful a ride for him as a plunge down a giant waterfall would be for us.

But he was already so near to the edge that he could not stop. The boat raced on, and the poor tin soldier held himself as stiffly as he could. No one could say of him that he even blinked an eye. All at once the little vessel whirled round three or four times and filled with water to the brim; what could it do but sink! The tin soldier stood in water up to his neck, deeper and deeper sank the boat, softer and softer grew the paper, until at last the water closed over the soldier's head. He thought of the lovely little dancer whom he would never see again, and in his ears rang the words of a song:

> *Onward, onward, warrior,*
> *Meet thy fate; show no fear.*

Then the paper boat collapsed altogether. Out fell the tin soldier — and was at once swallowed up by a fish.

Oh, how dark it was in the fish's stomach! It was even worse than the tunnel, and much more cramped. But the tin soldier's courage was quite unchanged; there he lay, steadfast as ever, his musket still on his shoulder. The fish swam wildly to and fro, twisted and turned, and then became still. Something flashed through like a streak of lightning — then all around was cheerful daylight. A voice cried out, "The tin soldier!"

The fish had been caught, taken to market, sold and carried into the kitchen, where the cook had cut it open with a large knife. Now she picked up the soldier, holding him round his waist between her finger and thumb, and took him into the living room, so that all the family could see and admire the remarkable

character who had traveled back in a fish. But the tin soldier was not proud; he thought nothing of it.

They stood him up on the table, and there — well, the world is full of wonders. He saw that he was in the very same room where his adventures had started; there were the same children; there were the same toys; there was the fine paper castle with the

graceful little dancer at the door. She was still poised on one leg, with the other raised high in the air. Ah, she was steadfast too. The tin soldier was deeply moved; he would have liked to weep tin tears, only that would not have been soldierly behavior. He looked at her and she looked at him, but not a word passed between them.

And then a strange thing happened. One of the small boys picked up the tin soldier and threw him in the stove. He had no reason for doing this; it must have been the fault of the snuffbox goblin.

The tin soldier stood framed in a blaze of light. The heat was intense, but whether this came from the fire or from his burning love he could not tell. His bright colors were now completely gone, but whether they had faded on the journey or through his sorrow, none could say. He looked at the little dancer, and she looked at him; he felt that he was melting, but he still stood steadfast, shouldering arms. Suddenly the door flew open; a gust of air caught the pretty little paper dancer, and she flew like a sylph right into the stove, straight to the waiting tin soldier; there she flashed into flame and was gone.

Soon the soldier melted down to a lump of tin, and the next day, when the maid raked out the ashes, she found him — in the shape of a little tin heart. What remained of the dancer?

Only her spangle, and
that was black as soot.

Rag Bag

Ruth Ainsworth

An unusual story, this, about a fairy child who envies the pleasure that a human child gets from her dolls and who wants one of them for herself. It's a tale about different kinds of magic, really. What the eerie, pathetic but rather stupid fairy lacks, and Carol possesses, is a special gift granted to humans (or some of them, and even then not used nearly enough) — and that's imagination. How much is real, how much is pretend? Carol seems to understand this very well.

Ruth Ainsworth's stories were almost always aimed at the very young. Born in 1908 on the Suffolk coast and later moving to Northumberland, she reflects in her tales their wild areas, still unspoiled in her time. In her many tales, Ainsworth excels at bringing to readers "the timeless camaraderie of children, animals, and toys." There are not many storytellers today so skillful in her particular field or with so tireless an imagination.

Carol was playing halfway up the stairs. She was sitting on one stair, and on the next stair up she had spread out three little blue cups and three little blue saucers and three little blue plates. Also a milk jug and a sugar bowl. On the next step up, above the tea set, sat her three dolls, their legs stuck stiffly out and their faces smiling with anticipation.

There was Rag Bag, the oldest doll, who had belonged to Carol's mother, and before that to her grandmother. Her looks were not improved by the many adventures she had had in her long life, but all the hugs and kisses she had had gave her face a contented expression. She was dearly loved and loved everybody else in return.

The next was Saucy Sally, a very smart doll with fashionable clothes. She had real hair and black patent slippers. She carried a handbag that closed with a zip.

The third doll was a boy called Jolly Roger, or Roger for short. He had a sailor hat on the back of his curly head and a sailor's blouse with a wide collar. He had flappy blue trousers and gold earrings in his ears.

Carol loved all her dolls but she had a special feeling for Rag Bag because she could do something the others couldn't manage. She could speak, though she only spoke when alone with Carol and the other dolls, never in front of any grown-up person. And no one could call her really talkative. She simply spoke if she had something to say.

"Here is your tea, Rag Bag. Plenty of milk, just as you like it."

Rag Bag's smile spread even farther.

"And here is yours, Saucy Sally. Three lumps of sugar."

Saucy Sally gave a small polite bow.

"And here is yours, Roger. A good strong cup for a sturdy sailor boy."

Roger took his cup and saluted.

"Butter fingers!" said Carol, as the cup tilted. "How you manage onboard ship with the deck tilting beats me." Then the food was handed round. Rag Bag took a piece of bread and butter, as she had been taught. Saucy Sally bit daintily into a doughnut. Roger took a ship's biscuit. He made dreadful crunching noises, but if you have ever eaten a ship's biscuit you'll know that he couldn't help it. They are so very, very hard. Roger kept looking over his shoulder, so he made a lot of crumbs on the carpet.

"Roger," said Carol, watching him, "have you seen something? Has she appeared again?"

Roger nodded. The others turned their heads too and looked back up the stairs.

"She seems to have gone," said Carol. "That's a good thing."

The dolls looked relieved and went on eating, but Carol kept watch on the landing above, out of the corner of her eye.

Silently, out of nothing at all, a queer little person gradually took shape. She was a small child, but her white face was not childlike. Her clothes were not suitable for a child either. They seemed to be a bundle of dark rags. She had a large, lumpy nose and a very round chin. She was not of this world.

"Go away!" said Carol. "Please go back where you came from and don't visit us again. Not ever."

The queer child gathered up her dark, trailing skirt and ran away nimbly on bare feet.

Carol's voice was shaky with fear, but she comforted the dolls as well as she could.

"I think it must be one of the Little People, or rather one of their children, who has got into the house by mistake. We've seen her three times, haven't we? Looking through the window.

Peering into the pram. And rummaging in the toy box."

"This makes four," said Carol, speaking for Roger.

⁓

The next time Carol saw anything strange, she was alone in the hall and came face to face with the bundly child. It was no good saying go away. The Fairy Child stood firm. She was not going to budge.

"Do you want something?" said Carol at last.

"Yes, I do. And if you don't give it to me, I'll take it."

"What is it?"

"It's a doll. We Fairy Children don't have dolls. I'll have one of yours."

"You can't. I can't spare one. They are mine. I'll make you a doll. Come tomorrow and she'll be ready."

Carol had an older sister called Kate, and Kate helped her to make a doll, or she could never have managed alone.

"What do you want another doll *for*?" asked Kate.

"For a sort of present. A secret present," explained Carol.

The doll was made out of a clothes' peg, with one side of the head blacked with shoe polish for hair, and

50

a face drawn on the other side. Kate made a shawl out of a handkerchief and a skirt out of an egg cozy.

"Will she do?" asked Kate, holding her at arm's length.

"She'll do beautifully. Thank you, Kate," said Carol.

The next day the Fairy Child appeared, suddenly and silently, as usual.

"Where is my doll?" she inquired abruptly.

"Here," said Carol, handing her over. "Be kind to her."

"She'll do," said the Fairy Child, ungraciously.

"Don't please come back," begged Carol.

"I might!" said the Child with a teasing laugh.

Carol and her dolls were left in peace for some days and they began to feel safe and comfortable, and stopped looking in dark corners and behind things. Then, on a Saturday morning, the Fairy Child appeared again, with no warning. One minute she wasn't there. The next minute she was. She came close to Carol and caught hold of her arm. Carol felt the chill of her sharp fingers through her jersey.

"I want a handbag for my doll."

Saucy Sally moved behind Rag Bag, hiding her handbag. Roger was shaking so much his earrings jingled.

"I'll try to make one, if you give me time," said Carol.

"Tomorrow?" asked the Child. "I don't like waiting."

"Tomorrow, then," said Carol doubtfully.

Once more she had to ask Kate to help her, but this time Kate was not so willing to help. She was keeping a diary and drawing a picture to illustrate every day, and that took most of her leisure. But she realized that Carol was upset about something and she said she would have a go at making a handbag.

In the end, Kate cut the thumb off an old glove and tied a piece of ribbon round the mouth for a handle. Then they added a drop of their mother's scent.

The next day the Fairy Child appeared. She did not think much of the handbag, but she liked the scent, and went off sniffing and grumbling.

Once more there was peace in the house, but not for long. The unwelcome visitor came again, swinging her doll carelessly, and this time she asked, indeed demanded, "earrings for my doll."

Roger, very conscious of his earrings, crept under the table and pretended he wasn't there.

"I could draw some on with my colored pens," suggested Carol. "What color would you like?"

"That wouldn't do at all. They must swing and jingle. If you can't make me a proper doll I shall have to take one of yours. You can surely spare *one.*"

"Well, I can't. They are my children. Could your mother spare one of her children?"

"I expect she could. She has ten other children and she can't count beyond double figures. It's a family failing. She'd never know I'd gone."

"Then I'm not like your mother," replied Carol. "But I'll see what I can do. You'll have to leave her with me till tomorrow. I'll take great care of her."

"She's very tough," said the Fairy Child, handing the peg doll over upside down. "She'll come to no harm. She gets more kicks than kisses. I pinch her much more often than I pet her."

"You don't deserve to have a doll if you don't know how to treat her!" Carol's eyes filled with tears as she cradled the little peg doll in her arms. "Kicks indeed," she muttered. "I'd like to kick you."

"I heard what you whispered," said the Fairy Child,

"and I shan't forget it. We Little People have good ears and good memories."

Carol knew that even Kate would be no help in making earrings but her father might be able to do something. He had a tool-box full of all kinds of tools. When he came home she asked him: "Daddy. Can you make earrings for a doll?"

"I could try, I suppose. Where's the doll?"

Carol gave him the little peg doll.

"I'll have to drill two holes and the wood might split. Keep your fingers crossed. I'll have a go when I've had my tea."

The wood didn't split and by bedtime the peg doll was wearing wire earrings that looked like silver and jingled when she shook her head.

Next time the bundly Child appeared, Carol's three dolls hid themselves in the toy box. There was no telling what she would take a fancy to next, Roger's anchor buttons or Saucy Sally's shiny shoes. Only Rag Bag was not worried. She was so old and shabby that no one would take any notice of her.

The Fairy Child jingled the new earrings. Remarked that she would have preferred gold. Scowled at Carol, and disappeared.

"Perhaps we've seen the last of her," sighed Carol.

"Don't be too sure," said Rag Bag. "But whatever happens we'll get the better of her. We'll use our brains."

"Perhaps she has a good brain as well as a good memory?"

"Anyhow, she hasn't a heart. More pinching than petting, indeed."

The other dolls looked shocked. What a dreadful place the world seemed, beyond the walls of their safe, warm home, where they only knew kindness and gentle voices.

Weeks passed and there was no visit from the Fairy Child. Saucy Sally and Roger forgot all about her, but Rag Bag never forgot, though she kept her thoughts to herself. Carol sometimes shuddered when an unexpected shadow fell on her path. Then, one dull day in the garden, she found the Fairy Child was standing at her side. At first neither of them spoke.

"How is your doll?" asked Carol. "What have you called her?"

"Oh, that wooden peg creature." The Fairy Child laughed unpleasantly. "I got tired of her. I threw her in the dustbin."

"But why? She was so nice with her earrings and her smile and everything."

"Nice! I don't call her nice. I call her a stupid wooden image. She couldn't talk or sing or dance or eat or amuse me. She was useless."

"Couldn't you pretend she could do all those things? I pretend my dolls can do anything in the world. They can even fly, if I want them to."

"I never pretend. I don't know how to pretend. I don't want a doll if I have to pretend things. I want a real companion who can do everything that I can do. I want one of *your* dolls."

"But if you had one of my dolls," said Carol, "you'd still have to pretend. So you wouldn't be better pleased than you were with the peg doll."

"I don't believe you," said the Fairy Child angrily. "I've seen you having fun with your dolls – giving parties – having adventures. I often hear other voices besides yours. A very high voice and a very gruff voice. I know one is Sally and one is Roger. You aren't speaking the truth. They can do lots of things my stupid peg doll couldn't. That's why I threw her in the dustbin."

Carol opened her eyes in amazement. "But don't you understand," she explained. "It's all pretending. I speak in a high voice for Sally and a gruff one for Roger. It all seems real, but I'm only playing. Only pretending."

"I don't believe you," said the Fairy Child stubbornly.

Carol was very thankful that Rag Bag hadn't been mentioned because she really could speak.

There was the sound of footsteps approaching.

"I shall come back tomorrow and make my choice," said the Fairy Child, fading into a bush. "And it's no good trying to hide them because I shall find them. I can see through things."

"I thought I heard voices," said Carol's mother, coming along the path.

"I was playing," said Carol quickly, "with Rag Bag."

"I'm so glad you like Rag Bag," said her mother. "I loved her when I was your age, and so did Granny who had her first. She's such a comfortable creature."

"Did she ever talk to you when you were little?" asked Carol.

"What a strange question to ask. I know I pretended she could talk. It's so long ago, but I almost think she did. But she couldn't, could she?"

"I don't see why not," said Carol, giving Rag Bag a hug.

At bedtime, Rag Bag was nowhere to be seen. She always slept with Carol, snug in her arms with her head sharing the pillow, her bright yellow locks, which were getting thin with age, mixed with Carol's brown hair.

"How awful if that horrible child has stolen her away," said Carol, almost in tears.

"She said 'tomorrow,'" comforted Roger.

"And she usually does what she says," added Saucy Sally.

Just then, Rag Bag appeared, out of breath, as she had been running. The pockets of her apron were bulging with rowan berries. Her feet were wet.

"Where ever have you been?" asked Carol.

"I've been in the garden, preparing for the worst," said Rag Bag, climbing

into bed, wet feet and bulging pockets and all.

During the night, Rag Bag freed herself very slowly and carefully from Carol's arms and crept out of bed. She spent a long time sitting on the floor in the moonlight, Carol's work basket beside her, busy with a needle and a long length of thread. When she had finished what she was doing she tidied the work basket, put the lid on, and crept back into Carol's warm bed.

The next day, no one could settle to anything. Carol started every time there was an unexpected sound, and if a door banged, or someone sneezed, the dolls dived behind curtains.

When the Fairy Child appeared, no one was expecting her. She just grew up out of the floor, suddenly and silently, like a mushroom. No one ran away or tried to hide. They all kept still as stones.

"I said I'd be here today and here I am," she said in her disagreeable voice. "I've decided to have Rag Bag. I know there's something special about her and I mean to find out what it is. There's some mystery I don't understand."

"You can't. I love her so much. I've always had her since I was a baby." Carol was almost crying.

"Then it's time someone else had a turn. Come on, Rag Bag."

Carol snatched Rag Bag up in her arms, but Rag Bag whispered in her ear: "Let me go. I'll come back. Trust me and don't fret."

Carol slowly let go and the Fairy Child took her remarkably gently in her arms and they vanished through the door without opening it.

"We must be brave," said Carol in a shaky voice. "Rag Bag said she'd come back and so she will. Let's play snakes and ladders to cheer ourselves up. You can have first turn, Roger."

"Where are you taking me?" asked Rag Bag as the Fairy Child hurried along, still holding her gently.

"To the Fairy Hill where you'll spend the rest of your life. So you *can* talk, after all. You can talk perfectly. Carol was telling lies."

"No, she wasn't telling lies," said Rag Bag indignantly. "She said Saucy Sally and Roger couldn't talk and they can't. Not a word. She has to talk for them."

"Then why is it you can talk? Tell me that."

"I was made by a wise old woman who stitched some magic into me," said Rag Bag. "And it's still there."

"I wish you could walk as well. My arms are aching."

"Then why not have a rest?" said Rag Bag.

"I will. You can tell me a story."

"All right," agreed Rag Bag.

The Fairy Child lay down under a tree, because they

were passing through a wood, and closed her eyes. Rag Bag began a very uninteresting story about two bears called Nid and Nod. Soon the Fairy Child was fast asleep.

Then Rag Bag worked quickly. First she whispered a sleep charm into the Fairy Child's ear to make sure that she would not wake for a long time.

> *"Sleep, sleep,*
> *Deep, deep,*
> *Count a thousand sheep*
> *Into the fold."*

She repeated this three times. Then she took out of her apron pocket the long, long string of rowan berries that she had threaded during the night. She laid the string in a circle round the sleeping Child. Then she set off home. She might easily have lost the way, but every creature in the wood helped her.

"Over here, over here," squeaked a mouse.

"That way, that way," whistled a bird.

"Over the log, over the log," snuffled a hedgehog.

"Cross the stream, cross the stream," croaked a frog.

So she found her way safely and easily, and ended up in her own garden. Carol was sitting on the swing with the dolls in her lap. The swing was just moving. All three looked the picture of misery.

"She said she'd come back," said Roger, trying to sound comforting. "She'll come in the end."

"But I want her now. This very minute," said Carol. "Oh, Rag Bag, why did I let you go so easily? There must have been something I could have done."

"Well, here I am, just as I said," and Rag Bag climbed onto Carol's lap with the other two. They all hugged and kissed each other, and when Rag Bag could speak, she related her adventures. She described how she had gathered the rowan berries and threaded them into a long string, because the Fairy Folk hate and fear the rowan tree and its fruits.

"When the Fairy Child wakes up," went on Rag Bag, "she won't be able to move. She won't dare to cross the rowan berry ring."

"Will she starve to death?" asked Carol. "I feel sorry for her."

"Oh no," said Rag Bag. "Some of her own people will

find her and they'll discover a way of moving the berries without actually touching them. Then she'll be free. But I shall be surprised if she shows her face here again. She'll have had such a fright."

That night, when they were all in bed, Carol asked Rag Bag to tell them the sleepy story about Nid and Nod because they were far too excited to go to sleep. Rag Bag began it and it was so very dull that everyone was asleep in no time. Then, just to make sure, she whispered the sleep charm:

"Sleep, sleep,
Deep, deep,
Count a thousand sheep
Into the fold."

Vasilissa, Baba Yaga, and the Little Doll

Retold by Naomi Lewis

Baba Yaga, great witch of Russian fairy tale, is also one of the great witches of all fairy tale — quite unmistakable with her hut mounted on hens' claws and her mortar and pestle (a heavy bowl and pounder used by cooks and chemists) for an air limousine. Only a witch of quality and of rare grim humor would think to fly around in anything so unlikely. But in this splendid story Vasilissa's doll is Baba Yaga's full match in magic! Friend, confidante, solver of problems that seem insoluble, this is the doll of everyone's secret wish.

There are many Baba Yaga stories, but this seems to me one of the best. The detail itself is magnificent. Those three horsemen of dawn, day, and night, for instance, and even the weird light that Baba Yaga, playing fair in her way, allows Vasilissa on her journey home. A marvelous tale.

In a far-off land in a far-off time, on the edge of a great forest, lived a girl named Vasilissa. Ah, poor Vasilissa! She was no more than eight years old when her mother died. But she had a friend, and that one was better than most. Who was this friend? A doll, a wooden doll.

As the mother lay ill she had called the child to her bedside. "Vasilissa," she said, "here is a little doll. Take good care of her, and whenever you are in great need, give her some food and ask for her help; she will tell you what to do. Take her, with my blessing; but remember, she is your secret; no one else must know of her at all. Now I can die content."

The father of Vasilissa grieved for a time, then married a new wife, thinking that she would care for the little girl. But did she indeed! She had two daughters of her own, and not one of the three had a grain of love for Vasilissa. From early dawn to the last light of day, in the hot sun or the icy wind, they kept her toiling at all the hardest tasks, in or out of the house; never did she have a word of thanks. Yet whatever they set her to do was done, and done in time. For when she truly needed help she would set her doll on a ledge or table, give her a little food and drink, and tell the doll her troubles. With her help all was done.

One day in the late autumn the father had to leave for the town, a journey of many days. He set off at earliest dawn.

Darkness fell early. Rain beat on the cottage windows; the wind howled down the chimney — just the time for the wife to work a plan she had in mind. To each of the girls she gave a task: the first was set to making lace, the second to knitting stockings, Vasilissa to spinning.

"No stirring from your place, my girls, before you have done," said the woman. Then, leaving them a single candle, she went to bed.

The three worked on for a while, but the light was small, and flickered. One sister pretended to trim the wick and it went out altogether — just as the mother had planned.

"Now we're in trouble," said the girl. "For where's the new light to come from?"

"There's only one place," said her sister, "and that's from Baba Yaga."

"That's right," said the other. "But who's to go?

>*My needles shine;*
>>*The job's not mine."*

"I can manage too," said the other.

>*"My lace-pins shine;*
>>*The job's not mine.*

Vasilissa must go."

"Yes, Vasilissa must go!" they cried together. And they pushed her out of the door.

Now who was Baba Yaga? She was a mighty witch; her hut was set on claws, like the legs of giant hens. She rode in a mortar over the highest mountains, speeding it on with the pestle, sweeping away her traces with a broom. And she would crunch up in a trice any human who crossed her path.

But Vasilissa had a friend, and that one better than most. She took the doll from her pocket, and set some

bread before her. "Little doll," she said, "they are sending me into the forest to fetch a light from Baba Yaga's hut — and who has ever returned from there? Help me, little doll."

The doll ate, and her eyes grew bright as stars. "Have no fear," said she. "While I am with you nothing can do you harm. But remember — no one else must know of your secret. Now let us start."

How dark it was in the forest of towering trees! How the leaves hissed, how the branches creaked and moaned in the wind! But Vasilissa walked resolutely on, hour after hour. Suddenly, the earth began to tremble and a horseman thundered by. Both horse and rider were glittering white, hair and mane, swirling cloak and bridle too; and as they passed, the sky showed the first white light of dawn.

Vasilissa journeyed on, then again she heard a thundering noise, and a second horse and rider flashed into sight. Both shone red as scarlet, red as flame, swirling cloak and bridle too; as they rode beyond her view, the sun rose high. It was day.

On she walked, on and on, until she reached a clearing in the woods. In the center was a hut —

but the hut had feet; and they were the claws of hens. It was Baba Yaga's home, no doubt about that. All around was a fence of bones, and the posts were topped with skulls: a fearful sight in the fading light! And as she gazed, a third horseman thundered

past; but this time horse and rider were black and black, swirling cloak and bridle too. They vanished into the gloom, and it was night. But, as darkness fell, the eyes of the skulls lit up like lamps and everything in the glade could be seen as sharp as day.

Swish! Swoosh! Varoom! Varoom! As Vasilissa stood there, frozen stiff with fear, a terrible noise came from over the forest. The wind screeched, the leaves hissed — Baba Yaga was riding home in her huge mortar, using her pestle as an oar, sweeping away the traces with her broom. At the gate of the hut she stopped and sniffed the air with her long nose.

Baba Yaga was riding home in her huge mortar, using her pestle
as an oar, sweeping away the traces with her broom.

"Phoo! Phoo! I smell Russian flesh!" she croaked. "Who's there? Out you come!"

Vasilissa took courage, stepped forward, and made a low curtsy.

"It is I, Vasilissa. My sisters sent me for a light, since ours went out."

"Oh, so that's it!" said the witch. "I know those girls, and their mother too. Well, nothing's for nothing, as they say; you must work for me for a while, then we'll see about the light." She turned to the hut and sang in a high shrill screech:

"Open gates! Open gates!
Baba Yaga waits."

The weird fence opened; the witch seized the girl's arm in her bony fingers and pushed her into the hut. "Now," said she, "get a light from the lamps outside," — she meant the skulls — "and serve my supper. It's in the oven, and the soup's in the cauldron there." She lay down on a bench while Vasilissa carried the food to the table until she was quite worn out, but she dared not stop. And the witch devoured more than ten strong men could have eaten — whole geese and hens and roasted pigs; loaf after loaf; huge buckets of beer and wine: cider and Russian kvass. At last, all that remained was a crust of bread.

"There's your supper, girl," said the witch. "But you must earn it, mind; I don't like greed. While I'm off tomorrow you must clear out the yard; it hasn't been touched for years, and it quite blocks out the view. Then you must sweep the hut, wash the linen, cook the dinner — and mind you cook enough; I was half-starved tonight. Then — for I'll have no lazybones around — there's another little job. You see that sack? It's full of black beans, wheat, and poppy seed, some other things too, I dare say. Sort them out into their separate lots,

and if a single one is out of place, woe betide! Into the cauldron you shall go, and I'll crunch you up for breakfast in a trice." So saying, she lay down by the stove and was instantly fast asleep. Snorrre ...Snorrre ... It was a horrible sound.

Vasilissa took the doll from her pocket and gave her the piece of bread. "Little doll," said she, "how am I to do all these tasks? Or even one of them? How can a little doll like you help now? We are lost indeed."

"Vasilissa," said the doll, "again I tell you, have no fear. Say your prayers and go to sleep. Tomorrow knows what is hidden from yesterday."

She slept – but she woke early, before the first glimmer of day. Where should she start on the mountain of work? Then she heard a thundering of hoofs; white horse and white rider flashed past the window – suddenly it was dawn. The light in the skulls' eyes dwindled and went out. Then the poor girl hid in the shadows, for she saw Baba Yaga get to her feet – Creak! Creak! – and shuffle to the door. There, the witch gave a piercing whistle, and mortar, pestle, and broom came hurtling toward her, stopping where she stood. In she stepped, off she rode, over treetops, through the clouds, using the pestle like an oar, sweeping away her traces with the broom. Just as she soared away, the red horse and red rider thundered past: suddenly it was day, and the sun shone down.

Vasilissa turned away from the window, but what was this? She could not believe her eyes.

Every task was done. The yard was cleared, the linen washed, the grains and the seeds were all in separate bins, the dinner was set to cook. And there was the little doll, waiting to get back in her pocket. "All you need to do," said the doll, "is to set the table and serve it all, hot and hot, when she returns. But keep your wits about you all the same, for she's a sly one."

The winter daylight faded fast; again there was a thundering of hoofs; black horse, black rider sped through the glade and were gone. Darkness fell, and the eyes of the skulls once more began to glow. And then, with a swish and a roar, down swept the mortar, out stepped Baba Yaga.

"Well, girl, why are you standing idle? You know what I told you."

"The work is all done, Granny."

Baba Yaga looked and looked but done it all was. So she sat down, grumbling and mumbling, to eat her supper. It was good, very good: it put her in a pleasant humor, for a witch.

"Tell me, girl, why do you sit there as if you were dumb?"

"Granny, I did not dare to speak — but, now, if you permit it, may I ask a question?"

"Ask if you will, but remember that not every question leads to good. The more you know, the older you grow."

"Well, Granny, can you tell me, who is the white rider on the white horse, the one who passed at dawn?"

"He is my Bright Morning, and he brings the earliest light."

"Then who is the rider all in red on the flame-red horse?"

"Ah, he is my Fiery Sun and brings the day."

"And who is the horseman all in black on the coal-black horse?"

"He is my Dark Night. All are my faithful servants. Now I shall ask *you* a question; mind you answer me properly. How did you do all those tasks I set you?"

Vasilissa recalled her mother's words, never to tell the secret of the doll.

"My mother gave me a blessing before she died, and that helps me when in need."

"A blessing! I want no blessed children here! Out you get! Away! Away!" And she pushed her through the door. "You've earned your pay — now take it." She took down one of the gate-post skulls, fixed it on a stick, and thrust it into Vasilissa's hand. "Now — off!"

Vasilissa needed no second bidding. She hastened on, her path now lit by the eyes of the fearful lamp. And so, at last, she was home.

"Why have you taken so long?" screamed the mother and the sisters. They had been in darkness ever since she left. They had gone in every direction to borrow a light, but once it was inside in the house, every flame went out. So they seized the skull with joy.

But the glaring eyes stared back; wherever they turned they could not escape the scorching rays. Soon, all that remained of the three was a little ash. Then the light of the skull went out for ever; its task was done.

Vasilissa buried it in the garden, and a bush of red roses sprang up on the spot. She did not fear to be alone, for the little doll kept her company. And when her father returned, rejoicing to see her, this tale she told him, just as it has been told to you.

Rocking Horse Land

Laurence Housman

Wild-eyed, restless, moving with urgent energy yet held in the same place, the rocking horse always suggests the need for escape and for soaring flight, a need that is exactly caught in this fine mysterious tale.

Laurence Housman, the younger brother of A. E. Housman who wrote A SHROPSHIRE LAD, *lived for nearly a century (1865–1959) and had several professions. He began as an artist and illustrator, became art critic of the* MANCHESTER GUARDIAN, *and then realized that writing was much more to his taste and skill. His earliest writings were fairy tales of a haunting, melodious charm, and* ROCKING HORSE LAND *(1894) is one of them. If it seems to have a flavor very much like one of Oscar Wilde's resounding fairy tales this is hardly surprising, for it belongs to the same mood and period.*

Little Prince Freedling woke up with a jump, and sprang out of bed into the sunshine. He was five years old that morning, by all the clocks and calendars in the kingdom; and the day was going to be beautiful. Every golden minute was precious. He was dressed and out of the room before the attendants knew that he was awake.

In the antechamber stood piles on piles of glittering presents; when he walked among them they came up to the measure of his waist. His fairy godmother had sent him a toy with the most humorous effect. It was labeled, "Break me and I shall turn into something else." So every time he broke it he got a new toy more beautiful than the last. It began by being a hoop, and from that it ran on, while the Prince broke it incessantly for the space of one hour, during which it became by turn — a top, a Noah's ark, a skipping-rope, a man-of-war, a box of bricks, a picture puzzle, a pair of stilts, a drum, a trumpet, a kaleidoscope, a steam engine, and nine hundred and fifty other things exactly.

Then he began to grow discontented, because it would never turn into the same thing again; and after having broken the man-of-war he wanted to get it back again. Also, he wanted to see if the steam engine would go inside the Noah's ark; but the toy would never be two things at the same time either. This was very unsatisfactory. He thought his fairy godmother ought to have sent him two toys, out of which he could make combinations.

At last he broke it once more, and it turned into a kite; and while he was flying the kite he broke the string, and the kite went sailing away up into the nasty blue sky, and was never heard of again.

Then Prince Freedling sat down and howled at his fairy godmother; what a dissembling lot fairy godmothers were, to be sure! They were always setting traps to make their godchildren unhappy. Nevertheless, when told to, he took up his pen and wrote her a nice little note, full of bad spelling and tarradiddles, to say what a happy birthday he was spending in breaking up the beautiful toy she had sent him.

Then he went to look at the rest of the presents, and found it quite refreshing to break a few that did not send him giddy by turning into anything else.

Suddenly his eyes became fixed with delight; alone, right at the end of the room, stood a great black rocking horse. The saddle and bridle were hung with tiny gold bells and balls of coral; and the horse's tail and mane flowed till they almost touched the ground.

The Prince scampered across the room, and threw his arms around the beautiful creature's neck. All its bells jingled as the head swayed gracefully down; and the prince kissed it between the eyes. Great eyes they were, the color of fire, so wonderfully bright, it seemed they must be really alive, only they did not move, but gazed continuously with a set stare at the tapestry-hung walls on which were figures of armed knights riding to battle.

So Prince Freedling mounted to the back of his rocking horse; and all day long he rode and shouted to the figures of the armed knights, challenging them to fight, or leading them against the enemy.

At length, when it came to be bedtime, weary of so much glory, he was lifted down from the saddle and carried away to bed.

In his sleep Freedling still felt his black rocking horse swinging to and fro under him, and heard the melodious chime of its bells, and, in the land of dreams, saw a great country open before him, full of the sound of the battle cry and the hunting horn calling him to strange perils and triumphs.

In the middle of the night he grew softly awake, and his heart was full of love for his black rocking horse. He crept gently out of bed: he would go and look at it where it was standing so grand and still in the next room, to make sure it was all safe and not afraid of being by itself in the dark night. Parting the door-hangings he passed through into the wide hollow chamber beyond, all littered about with toys.

The moon was shining in through the window, making a square cistern of light upon the floor. And then, all at once, he saw that the rocking horse had moved from the place where he had left it! It had crossed the room, and was standing close to the window, with its head toward the night, as though watching the movement of the clouds and the trees swaying in the wind.

The Prince could not understand how it had been moved so; he was a little bit afraid, and stealing timidly across, he took hold of the bridle to comfort himself with the jangle of its bells. As he came close, and looked up into the dark solemn face, he saw that the eyes were full of tears and, reaching up, felt one fall warm against his hand.

"Why do you weep, my Beautiful?" said the Prince.

The rocking horse answered, "I weep because I am a prisoner, and not free. Open the window, Master, and let me go!"

"But if I let you go I shall lose you," said the Prince. "Cannot you be happy here with me?"

"Let me go," said the horse, "for my brothers call me out of Rocking Horse Land; I hear my mare whinnying to her foals; and they all cry, seeking me through the ups and hollows of my native fastnesses! Sweet Master, let me go this night, and I will return to you when it is day!"

Then Freedling said, "How shall I know that you will return: and what name shall I call you by?"

And the rocking horse answered, "My name is Rollonde. Search my mane till you find in it a white hair; draw it out and wind it upon one of your fingers; and so long as you have it so wound you are my master; and wherever I am I must return at your bidding."

So the Prince drew down the rocking horse's head and, searching the mane, he found the white hair and wound it upon his finger and tied it. Then he kissed Rollonde between the eyes, saying, "Go, Rollonde, since I love you and wish you to be happy; only return to me when it is day!" And so saying, he threw open the window to the stir of the night.

Then the rocking horse lifted his dark head and neighed aloud for joy and, swaying forward with a mighty circling motion, rose full into the air and sprang out into the free world before him.

Freedling watched how with plunge and curve he went over the bowed trees; and again he neighed into the darkness of the night, then swifter than wind he disappeared in the distance. And faintly from far away came a sound of the neighing of many horses answering him.

Then the rocking horse rose full into the air and
sprang out into the free world before him.

Then the Prince closed the window and crept back to bed: and all night long he dreamed strange dreams of Rocking Horse Land. There he saw smooth hills and valleys that rose and sank without a stone or a tree to disturb the steel-like polish of their surface, slippery as glass, and driven over by a strong wind; and over them, with a sound like the humming of bees, flew the rocking horses. Up and down, up and down, with bright manes streaming like colored fires and feet motionless behind and before, went the swift pendulum of their flight. Their long bodies bowed and rose; their heads worked to give impetus to their going; they cried, neighing to each other over hill and valley, "Which of us shall be first? Which of us shall be first?" After them the mares with their tall foals came spinning to watch, crying also among themselves, "Ah! Which shall be first?"

"Rollonde, Rollonde is first!" shouted the Prince, clapping his hands as they reached the goal; and at that, all at once, he woke and saw it was broad day. Then he ran and threw open the window and, holding out the finger that carried the white hair, cried, "Rollonde, Rollonde, come back, Rollonde!"

Far away he heard an answering sound; and in another moment there came the great rocking horse himself, dipping and dancing over the hills. He crossed the woods and cleared the palace wall at a bound and, floating in through the window, dropped to rest at Prince Freedling's side, rocking gently to and fro as though panting from the strain of his long flight.

"Now are you happy?" asked the Prince as he caressed him.

"Ah! Sweet Prince," said Rollonde, "ah, kind Master!" And then he said no more, but became the still

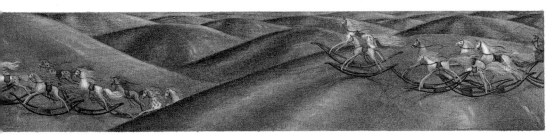

staring rocking horse of the day before, with fixed eyes and rigid limbs, which could do nothing but rock up and down with a jangling of sweet bells so long as the Prince rode him.

That night Freedling came again when all was still in the palace; and now as before Rollonde had moved from his place and was standing with his head against the window, waiting to be let out. "Ah, dear Master," he said, so soon as he saw the Prince coming, "let me go this night also, and surely I will return with day."

So again the Prince opened the window and watched him disappear and heard from far away the neighing of the horses in Rocking Horse Land calling to him. And in the morning, with the white hair round his finger, he called, "Rollonde, Rollonde!" and Rollonde neighed and came back to him, dipping and dancing over the hills.

Now this same thing happened every night; and every morning the horse kissed Freedling, saying, "Ah! Dear Prince and kind Master," and became stock still once more.

So a year went by, till one morning Freedling woke up to find it was his sixth birthday. And as six is to five, so were the presents he received on his sixth birthday for magnificence and multitude to the presents he had received the year before. His fairy godmother had sent him a bird, a real live bird; but when he pulled its tail it became a lizard, and when he pulled the lizard's tail it became a mouse, and when he pulled the mouse's tail it became a cat. Then he did very much want to see if the cat would eat the mouse and, not being able to have them both, he got rather vexed with his fairy godmother. However, he pulled the cat's tail and the cat became a dog, and when he pulled the dog's tail the dog became a goat; and so it went on till he got to a cow. And he pulled the cow's tail and it became a camel, and he pulled the camel's tail and it became an elephant, and still not being contented, he pulled the elephant's tail and it became a guinea pig. Now a guinea pig has no tail to pull, so it remained a guinea pig, while Prince Freedling sat down and howled at his fairy godmother.

But the best of all his presents was the one given to him by the King, his father. It was a most beautiful horse, for, said the King, "You are now old enough to learn to ride."

So Freedling was put upon the horse's back and, from having ridden so long upon his rocking horse, he learned to ride perfectly in a single day and was declared by all the courtiers to be the most perfect equestrian that was ever seen.

Now these praises and the pleasure of riding a real horse so occupied his thoughts that that night he forgot all about Rollonde and, falling fast asleep, dreamed of nothing but real horses and horsemen going to battle. And so it was the next night too.

But the night after that, just as he was falling asleep, he heard someone sobbing by his bed, and a voice saying, "Ah! Dear Prince and kind Master, let me go, for my heart breaks for a sight of my native land." And there stood his poor rocking horse, Rollonde, with tears falling out of his beautiful eyes onto the white coverlet.

Then the Prince, full of shame at having forgotten his friend, sprang up and threw his arms round his neck saying, "Be of good cheer, Rollonde, for now surely I will let thee go!" and he ran to the window and opened it for the horse to go through.

"Ah, dear Prince and kind Master!" said Rollonde.

Then he lifted his head and neighed so that the whole palace shook and, swaying forward till his head almost touched the ground, he sprang out into the night and away toward Rocking Horse Land.

Then Prince Freedling, standing by the window, thoughtfully unloosed the white hair from his finger and let it float away into the darkness, out of sight of his eye or reach of his hand.

"Good-bye, Rollonde," he murmured softly, "brave Rollonde, my own good Rollonde! Go and be happy in your own land since I, your Master, was forgetting to be kind to you." And far away he heard the neighing of horses in Rocking Horse Land.

Many years after, when Freedling had become King in his father's stead, the fifth birthday of the Prince, his son, came to be celebrated; and there on the morning of the day, among all the presents that covered the floor of the chamber, stood a beautiful foal rocking horse, black, with deep-burning eyes.

No one knew how it had come there, or whose present it was, till the King himself came to look at it.

And when he saw it, so like the old Rollonde he had loved as a boy, he smiled and, stroking its dark mane, said softly in its ear, "Art thou, then, the son of Rollonde?"

And the foal answered him, "Ah, dear Prince and kind Master!" but never a word more.

Then the King took the little Prince, his son, and told him the story of Rollonde as I have told it here; and at the end he went and searched in the foal's mane till he found one white hair and, drawing it out, he wound it about the little Prince's finger, bidding him guard it well and be ever a kind master to Rollonde's son.

The Town in the Library

E. Nesbit

Besides her long books for the young, such as THE RAILWAY CHILDREN *and* FIVE CHILDREN AND IT, E. Nesbit (1858-1924) wrote a number of short stories. The extraordinary story here has close links with her own life.

To begin with, the Rosamund and Fabian of THE TOWN IN THE LIBRARY were part of her own family — they were the third and fourth of her five children. (E. Nesbit is the mother in the tale.) More than this, the making of an imaginary town scene out of any objects around was her own invention, and was very much part of her children's lives. The whole thing started when one of the little boys was trying to make an Indian fort out of building bricks and could not get the right eastern atmosphere. E. Nesbit solved the problem with some chessmen, a brass bowl, and a book or two.

Rosamund and Fabian were left alone in the library. You may not believe this; but I advise you to believe everything I tell you, because it is true. Truth is stranger than story-books, and when you grow up you will hear people say this till you grow quite sick of listening to them: you will then want to write the strangest story that ever was — just to show that *some* stories can be stranger than truth.

Mother was obliged to leave the children alone, because Nurse was ill with measles, which seems a babyish thing for a grown-up nurse to have — but it is quite true. If I had wanted to make up anything I could have said she was ill of a broken heart or a brain fever, which always happens in books. But I wish to speak the truth even if it sounds silly. And it *was* measles.

Mother could not stay with the children, because it was Christmas Eve, and on that day a lot of poor old people came up to get their Christmas presents, tea and snuff, and flannel petticoats, and warm capes, and boxes of needles and cottons, and things like that. Generally the children helped to give out the presents, but this year Mother was afraid they might be going to have measles themselves, and measles is a nasty forward illness with no manners at all. You can catch it from a person before they know they've got it.

So the children were left alone. Before Mother went away she said, "Look here, dears, you may play with your bricks, or make pictures with your pretty blocks that kind Uncle Thomas gave you, but you must not touch the two top drawers of the bureau. Now don't forget. And if you're good you shall have tea with me, and perhaps there will be cake. Now you *will* be good, won't you?"

Fabian and Rosamund promised faithfully that they would be *very* good and that they would not touch the two top drawers, and Mother went away to see about the flannel petticoats and the tea and snuff and tobacco and things.

When the children were left alone, Fabian said, "I am going to be very good. I shall be much more good than Mother expects me to."

"We *won't* look in the drawers," said Rosamund, stroking the shiny top of the bureau.

"We won't even *think* about the insides of the drawers," said Fabian. He stroked the bureau too and his fingers left four long streaks on it, because he had been eating toffee.

"I suppose," he said presently, "we may open the two *bottom* drawers? Mother couldn't have made a mistake — could she?"

So they opened the two bottom drawers just to be sure that Mother hadn't made a mistake, and to see whether there was anything in the bottom drawers that they ought not to look at.

But the bottom drawer of all had only old magazines in it. And the next to the bottom drawer had a lot of papers in it. The children knew at once by the look of the papers that they belonged to Father's great work about the Domestic Life of the Ancient Druids and they knew it was not right — or even interesting — to try to read other people's papers.

So they shut the drawers and looked at each other, and Fabian said, "I think it would be right to play with the bricks and the pretty blocks that Uncle Thomas gave us."

But Rosamund was younger than Fabian, and she said, "I am tired of the blocks, and I am tired of Uncle Thomas. I would rather look in the drawers."

"So would I," said Fabian. And they stood looking at the bureau.

Perhaps you don't know what a bureau is — children learn very little at school nowadays — so I will tell you that a bureau is a kind of chest of drawers. Sometimes it has a bookcase on the top of it, and instead of the two little top corner drawers like the chest of drawers in a bedroom it has a sloping lid, and when it is quite open you pull out two little boards underneath — and then it makes a sort of shelf for people to write letters on. The shelf lies quite flat, and lets you see little drawers inside

107

with mother of pearl handles — and a row of pigeon holes — (which are not holes pigeons live in, but places for keeping the letters carrier-pigeons could carry round their necks if they liked). And there is very often a tiny cupboard in the middle of the bureau, with a pattern on the door in different colored woods. So now you know.

Fabian stood first on one leg and then on the other, till Rosamund said, "Well, you might as well pull up your socks."

So he did. His socks were always just like a concertina or a very expensive photographic camera, but he used to say it was not his fault, and I suppose he knew best.

Then he said, "I say, Rom! Mother only said we weren't to *touch* the two top drawers —"

"I *should* like to be good," said Rosamund.

"I *mean* to be good," said Fabian. "But if you took the little thin poker that is not kept for best you could put it through one of the brass handles and I could hold the other handle with the tongs. And then we could open the drawer without touching it."

"So we could! How clever you are, Fabe," said

Rosamund. And she admired her brother very much. So they took the poker and the tongs. The front of the bureau got a little scratched, but the top drawer came open, and there they saw two boxes with glass tops and narrow gold paper going all round; though you could only see paper shavings through the glass they knew it was soldiers. Besides these boxes there was a doll and a donkey standing on a green grass plot that had wooden wheels, and a little wickerwork doll's cradle, and some brass cannons, and a bag that looked like marbles, and some flags, and a mouse that seemed as though it moved with clockwork; only, of course, they had promised not to touch the drawer, so they could not make sure. They looked at each other, and Fabian said: "I wish it was tomorrow!"

You have seen that Fabian was quite a clever boy; and he knew at once that these were the Christmas presents which Santa Claus had brought for him and Rosamund. But Rosamund said, "Oh dear, I wish we hadn't!"

However, she consented to open the other drawer — without touching it, of course, because she had promised faithfully — and when, with the poker and tongs, the other drawer came open, there were large wooden boxes – the kind that hold raisins and figs – and round boxes with paper on – smooth on the top and folded in pleats round the edge; and the children knew what was inside without looking. Everyone knows what candied fruit looks like on the outside of the box. There were square boxes, too – the kind that have crackers in – with a cracker going off on the lid, very different in size and brightness from what it does really, for, as no doubt you know, a cracker very often comes in two quite calmly, without any pop at all, and then you only have the motto and the sweet, which is never nice. Of course, if there is anything else in the cracker, such as brooches or rings, you have to let the little girl who sits next to you at supper have it.

When they had pushed back the drawer Fabian said, "Let us pull out the writing drawer and make a castle."

So they pulled the drawer out and put it on the floor. Please do not try to do this if your father has a bureau, because it leads to trouble. It was only because this one was broken that they were able to do it.

Then they began to build. They had the two boxes

of bricks — the wooden bricks with the pillars and the colored glass windows, and the rational bricks which are made of clay-like tiles. When all the bricks were used up they got the pretty picture blocks that kind Uncle Thomas gave them, and they built with these; but one box of blocks does not go far. Picture blocks are only good for building, except just at first. When you have made the pictures a few times you know exactly how they go, and then what's the good? This is a fault which belongs to many very expensive toys. These blocks had six pictures — Windsor Castle with the Royal Standard hoisted; ducks in a pond, with a very handsome green and blue drake; Rebecca at the well; a snowball fight — but none of the boys knew how to chuck a snowball; the Harvest Home; and the Death of Nelson.

These did not go far, as I said. There are six times as few blocks as there are pictures, because every block has six sides. If you don't understand this it shows they don't teach arithmetic at your school, or else that you don't do your home lessons.

But the best of a library is the books. Rosamund and Fabian made up with books. They got Shakespeare in fourteen volumes, and Rollin's *Ancient History* and Gibbon's *Decline and Fall,* and *The Beauties of Literature* in fifty-six fat little volumes, and they built not only a castle, but a town — and a big town — that presently towered high above them on the top of the bureau.

"It's almost big enough to get into," said Fabian, "if we had some steps." So they made steps with the *British Essayists,* the *Spectator* and the *Rambler,* and the *Observer,* and the *Tatler;* and when the steps were done they walked up them.

You may think that they could not have walked up these steps and into a town they had built themselves, but I assure you people have often done it, and anyway this is a true story. They had made a lovely gateway with two fat volumes of Macaulay and Milton's poetical

works on top, and as they went through it they felt all the feelings that people have to feel when they are tourists and see really fine architecture. (Architecture means buildings, but it is a grander word, as you see.)

Rosamund and Fabian simply walked up the steps into the town they had built. Whether they got smaller or the town got larger, I do not pretend to say. When they had gone under the great gateway they found that they were in a street that they could not remember building. But they were not disagreeable about it, and they said it was a very nice street all the same.

There was a large square in the middle of the town, with seats, and there they sat down, in the town they had made, and wondered how they could have been so clever as to build it. Then they went to the walls of the town — high, strong walls built of the *Encyclopaedia* and the *Biographical Dictionary* — and far away over the brown plain of the carpet they saw a great thing like a square mountain. It was very shiny. And as they looked at it a great slice of it pushed itself out, and Fabian saw the brass handles shine, and he said: "Why, Rom, that's the bureau."

"It's larger than I want it to be," said Rosamund, who was a little frightened. And indeed it did seem to be an extra size, for it was higher than the town.

The drawer of the great mountain bureau opened slowly, and the children could see something moving inside; then they saw the glass lid of one of the boxes go slowly up till it stood on end and looked like one side of the Crystal Palace, it was so large — and inside the box they saw something moving. The shavings and tissue paper and the cotton-wool heaved and tossed like a sea when it is rough and you wish you had not come for a sail. And then from among the heaving whiteness came out a blue soldier, and another and another. They let themselves down from the drawer with ropes of shavings, and when they were all out there were fifty of them — foot soldiers with rifles and fixed bayonets, as well as a thin captain on a horse and a sergeant and a drummer.

The drummer beat his drum and the whole company formed fours and marched straight for the town. They seemed to be quite full-size soldiers — indeed, *extra large*.

The children were very frightened. They left the walls

and ran up and down the streets of the town trying to find a place to hide.

"Oh, there's our very own house," cried Rosamund at last; "we shall be safe there." She was surprised as well as pleased to find their own house inside the town they had built.

So they ran in, and into the library, and there was the bureau and the town they had built, and it was all small and quite the proper size. But when

they looked out of the window it was not their own street, but the one they had built; they could see two volumes of *The Beauties of Literature* and the head of Rebecca in the house opposite, and down the street was the Mausoleum they had built after the pattern given in the red and yellow book that went with the bricks. It was all very confusing.

Suddenly, as they stood looking out of the windows, they heard a shouting, and there were the blue soldiers coming along the street by twos, and when the Captain got opposite their house he called out, "Fabian! Rosamund! Come down!"

And they had to, for they were very much frightened.

Then the Captain said, "We have taken this town, and you are our prisoners. Do not attempt to escape, or I don't know what will happen to you."

The children explained that they had built the town, so they thought it was theirs; but the captain said very politely, "That doesn't follow at all. It's our town now. And I want provisions for my soldiers."

"We haven't any," said Fabian, but Rosamund nudged him, and said, "Won't the soldiers be very fierce if they are hungry?"

The Blue Captain heard her, and said, "You are quite right, little girl. If you have any food, produce it. It will be a generous act, and may stop any unpleasantness. My soldiers *are* very fierce. Besides," he added in a lower tone, speaking behind his hand, "you need only feed the soldiers in the usual way."

When the children heard this their minds were made up.

"If you do not mind waiting a minute," said Fabian, politely, "I will bring down any little things I can find."

Then he took his tongs, and Rosamund took the poker, and they opened the drawer where the raisins and figs and dried fruits were — for everything in the library in the town was just the same as in the library at home — and they carried them out into the big square where the Captain had drawn up his blue regiment. And here the soldiers were fed. I suppose you know how tin soldiers are fed? But children learn so little at school nowadays that I daresay you don't, so I will tell you. You just put a bit of the fig or raisin, or whatever it is, on the soldier's tin bayonet — or his sword, if he is a cavalry man — and you let it stay on till you are tired of playing at giving the soldiers rations, and then of course *you eat it for him*. This was the way in which Fabian and Rosamund fed the starving blue soldiers. But when they had done so, the soldiers were as hungry as ever.

So then the Blue Captain, who had not had anything, even on the point of his sword, said, "More, more, my gallant men are fainting for lack of food."

So there was nothing for it but to bring out the candied fruits, and to feed the soldiers with them. So Fabian and Rosamund stuck bits of candied apricot and fig and pear and cherry and beetroot on the tops of the soldiers' bayonets, and when every soldier had a piece they put a fat candied cherry on the officer's sword. Then the children knew the soldiers would be quiet for a few minutes, and they ran back into their own house and into the library to talk to each other about what they had better do, for they both felt that the blue soldiers were a very hard-hearted set of men.

"They might shut us up in the dungeons," said Rosamund, "and then Mother might lock us in, when she shut up the lid of the bureau, and we should starve to death."

"I think it's all nonsense," said Fabian. But when they looked out of the window there was the house with Windsor Castle and the head of Rebecca just opposite.

"If we could only find Mother," said Rosamund; but they knew without looking that Mother was not in the house that they were in then.

"I wish we had that mouse that looked like clockwork – and the donkey, and the other box of soldiers – perhaps they are red ones, and they would fight the blue and lick them – because redcoats are English and they always win," said Fabian.

And then Rosamund said, "Oh, Fabe, I believe we could go into *this* town, too, if we tried!"

So they went to the bureau drawer, and Rosamund got out the other box of soldiers and the mouse – it *was* a clockwork one – and the donkey with panniers, and put them in the town, while Fabian ate up a few odd raisins that had dropped on the floor.

When all the soldiers (they *were* red) were arranged on the ramparts of the little town, Fabian said, "I'm sure we can get into this town," and sure enough they did, just as they had done into the first one. And it was exactly the same sort of town as the other.

So now they were in a town built in a library in a house in a town built in a library in a house in a town called London — and the town they were in now had red soldiers in it and they felt quite safe, and the Union Jack was stuck up over the gateway. It was a stiff little flag they had found with some others in the bureau drawer; it was meant to be stuck in the Christmas pudding, but they had stuck it between two blocks and put it over the gate of their town. They walked about this town and found their own house, just as before, and went in, and there was the toy town on the floor; and you will see that they might have walked into that town also, but they saw that it was no good, and that they couldn't get out that way, but would only get deeper and deeper into a nest of towns in libraries in houses in towns in libraries in houses in towns in … and so on for always – something like Chinese puzzle boxes multiplied by millions and millions for ever and ever. And they did not like even to think of this, because of course they would be getting farther and farther from home every time. And when Fabian explained all this to Rosamund she said he made her head ache, and she began to cry.

Then Fabian thumped her on the back and told her not to be a little silly, for he was a very kind brother. And he said, "Come out and let's see if the soldiers can tell us what to do."

So they went out; but the red soldiers said they knew nothing but drill, and even the Red Captain said he really couldn't advise. Then they met the clockwork mouse. He was big like an elephant, and the donkey with panniers was as big as a mastodon or a megatherium. (If they teach you anything at school of course they have taught you all about the megatherium and the mastodon.)

121

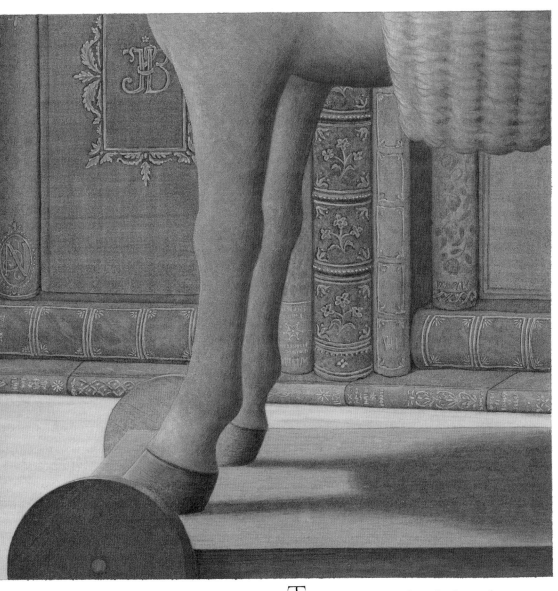

Then they met the clockwork mouse.
He was big like an elephant.

The Mouse kindly stopped to speak to the children, and Rosamund burst into tears again and said she wanted to go home.

The great Mouse looked down at her and said, "I am sorry for *you*, but your brother is the kind of child that overwinds clockwork mice the very first day he has them. I prefer to stay this size, and you to stay small."

Then Fabian said: "On my honor, I won't. If we get back home I'll give you to Rosamund. That is, supposing I get you for one of my Christmas presents."

The donkey with panniers said, "And you won't put coals in my panniers or unglue my feet from my green grass plot because I look more natural without wheels?"

"I give you my word," said Fabian. "I wouldn't think of such a thing."

"Very well," said the Mouse, "then I will tell you. It is a great secret, but there is only one way to get out of this kind of town. You — I hardly know how to explain — you — you just *walk out of the gate*, you know."

"Dear me," said Rosamund; "I never thought of that!"

So they all went to the gate of the town and walked out, and there they were in the library again. But when they looked out of the window the Mausoleum was still to be seen, and the terrible blue soldiers.

"What are we to do now?" asked Rosamund; but the clockwork mouse and the donkey with panniers were their proper size again now (or else the children had got bigger. It is no use asking me which, for I do not know), and so of course they could not speak.

"We must walk out of this town as we did out of the other," said Fabian.

"Yes," Rosamund said; "only this town is full of blue soldiers and I am afraid of them. Don't you think it would do if we *ran* out?"

So out they ran and down the steps that were made of the *Spectator* and the *Rambler* and the *Tatler* and the *Observer*. And directly they stood on the brown library carpet they ran to the window and looked out, and they saw — instead of the building with Windsor Castle and Rebecca's head in it — they saw their own road with the trees without any leaves and the man was just going along lighting the lamps with the stick that the gaslight pops out of, like a bird, to roost in the glass cage at the top of the lamppost.

So they knew that they were safe at home again.

And as they stood looking out they heard the library door open, and Mother's voice saying, "What a dreadful muddle! And what have you done with the raisins and the candied fruits?" And her voice was very grave indeed.

Now you will see that it was quite impossible for Fabian and Rosamund to explain to their mother what they had done with the raisins and things, and how they had been in a town in a library in a house in a town they had built in their own library with the books and the bricks and the pretty picture blocks kind Uncle Thomas gave them. Because they were much younger than I am, and even I have found it rather hard to explain.

So Rosamund said, "Oh, Mother, my head does ache so," and began to cry. And Fabian said nothing, but he, also, began to cry.

And Mother said, "I don't wonder your head aches, after all those sweet things." And she looked as if she would like to cry too.

"I don't know what Daddy will say," said Mother,

and then she gave them each a nasty powder and put them both to bed.

"I wonder what he *will* say," said Fabian just before he went to sleep.

"*I* don't know," said Rosamund, and, strange to say, they don't know to this hour what Daddy said. Because next day they both had measles, and when they got better everyone had forgotten about what had happened on Christmas Eve. And Fabian and Rosamund had forgotten just as much as everybody else. So I should never have heard of it but for the clockwork mouse. It was he who told me the story, just as the children told it to him in the town in the library in the house in the town they built in their own library with the books and the bricks and the pretty picture blocks which were given to them by kind Uncle Thomas. And if you do not believe the story it is not my fault: I believe every word the mouse said, for I know the good character of that clockwork mouse, and I know he could not tell an untruth even if he tried.

ACKNOWLEDGMENTS

The stories in this anthology were originally collected in THE SILENT PLAYMATE: A COLLECTION OF DOLL STORIES edited by Naomi Lewis (Victor Gollancz Ltd, 1979).

For permission to reprint copyright material in this book, the compiler and publisher gratefully acknowledge the following:

Rag Bag, an extract from UP THE AIRY MOUNTAIN by Ruth Ainsworth (William Heinemann Ltd). Reprinted by permission of R. F. Gilbert on behalf of the Estate of Ruth Ainsworth.

Rocking Horse Land, an extract from MOONSHINE AND CLOVER by Laurence Housman (Jonathan Cape Ltd). Reprinted by permission of Jonathan Cape Ltd on behalf of the Estate of Laurence Housman.

First U.S. edition 2000

Library of Congress Cataloging-in-Publication Data

Rocking horse land and other classic tales of dolls and toys / compiled by Naomi Lewis ;
pictures by Angela Barrett.—1st U.S. ed.

p.   cm.

Contents: The memoirs of a London doll / Mrs. Fairstar—The steadfast tin soldier / Hans Christian Andersen—Rag bag / Ruth Ainsworth—Vasilissa, Baba Yaga, and the little doll / retold by Naomi Lewis—Rocking horse land / Laurence Housman—The town in the library / E. Nesbit.

ISBN 0-7636-0897-1

1. Dolls—Juvenile fiction. 2. Children's stories. [1. Dolls—Fiction. 2. Toys—Fiction. 3. Short stories.]
I. Lewis, Naomi. II. Barrett, Angela, ill.

PZ5.R54   2000

[Fic]—dc21   00-035997

This book was typeset in Berkeley Old Style and Aquinas.
The illustrations were done in pencil and watercolor.

Printed in Belgium

2 4 6 8 10 9 7 5 3 1

Candlewick Press
2067 Massachusetts Avenue
Cambridge, Massachusetts 02140